49348

Hand-Me-Down House

MARY CROCKETT NORFLEET

Illustrated by Edgar Mallory

John Knox Press
RICHMOND, VIRGINIA

Second Printing 1967

Library of Congress Catalog Card Number: 62-18848
© M. E. Bratcher 1962
Printed in the United States of America

33-2340

To
ELINOR CURRY
with admiration
and with love

To the Reader

Every city is a changing city, made up of changing neighborhoods. Families buy houses. Children grow up and go to school. Later they go to work or to college. They marry and move away. Older people move out of houses into smaller apartments. Families with growing children move into bigger houses. Somebody moves somewhere every day.

In many cities, however, the words "changing neighborhood" have a very special meaning. Families who live in crowded sections move out to the ends of the bus lines where there is grass for their children's play and trees for the summer's shade.

This is the story of a family who moved into

a "changing neighborhood." It is especially the story of Martha who found it hard to love, and of Jakie who found it easy . . .

> At the same time came the disciples unto Jesus, saying, Who is the greatest in the kingdom of heaven?
>
> And Jesus called a little child unto him, and set him in the midst of them, and said, Verily I say unto you, Except ye be converted, and become as little children, ye shall not enter into the kingdom of heaven.
>
> Whosoever therefore shall humble himself as this little child, the same is greatest in the kingdom of heaven. And whoso shall receive one such little child in my name receiveth me.
>
> MATTHEW 18:1-5 (KJV)

Chapter 1

Moving day was over. James and Martha were swinging gently back and forth, back and forth, in the old-fashioned swing on the porch. Their little brother, Jakie, sat between them.

The house was a brick house, square and substantial, set well back in the middle of the big square lot. Everything about the house except the long front porch was square. There was a square front hall and a square living room. The dining room was square and so was the kitchen. Upstairs there were four corner bedrooms opening into a square center hall.

The four moving men came out the front door and slammed the screen behind them.

"Good-bye now, kids. Hope you like it here," said one of the men.

"Good-bye, and thanks for everything," said James.

The children watched as the men folded up the brown quilted covers they had used to protect the furniture. Two of the men sat on a pile of the quilts in the van. The other two climbed up into the cab. The motor started with a roar and the empty van rattled noisily down the bumpy street toward town.

James A. Anderson, Jr., stretched his long legs out and pushed the swing slowly back and forth. His sister Martha adjusted the rhythm of her swinging to his. Between them seven-year-old Jakie sat cross-legged and content to let his older brother and sister do the pushing. When his legs were down they did not quite reach the floor.

"I'm tired," said James.

"Me, too," said Martha.

"I'm tired too," said Jakie.

"That's a big joke," teased Martha. "How could you be tired?"

"I carried things."

"What things? Every time Daddy called you to get something, you were somewhere else."

Jakie appealed to James. "I did so carry things, didn't I, James? I carried lamps and stools. Didn't I, James?"

"Yes. You carried a lamp and a stool." James was truthful, if not very kind.

"Well, anyway, I carried things, and I'm tired," Martha said again.

"I'm tired too." James yawned and tilted his head back over the hard wooden slats of the creaking swing.

"Me, too," Jakie insisted. "I'm tired too."

"Oh, yes," said Martha, "I almost forgot. You carried things. Lamps and stools. Hundreds of lamps and hundreds of stools. One lamp and one stool, to be exact!"

"Mama! Mama!" Jakie jumped down and ran crying into the house. "They're tormenting me! They're tormenting me again!"

James turned to Martha.

"You shouldn't have done that," he said.

"Mother's tired and so is Daddy; and he has to go back to the office tonight."

"I know," Martha admitted, "but you were teasing him too."

"We ought to go in and help."

"Yes, I guess so," Martha agreed.

But they continued swinging, back and forth, back and forth. Through the open door they could hear the soft voice of their mother as she spoke gently to the little boy. Their father was arranging furniture, and they could hear him call out to their mother for directions as he placed the rugs and chairs.

Outside it was quiet. James and Martha could hear a few cars a block or two away, but they made a distant sound as in the background. All the clang and jangle were absorbed by the heavy foliage of the maple trees. Nearby there was the friendly sound of the creaking swing and the call of the swallows above the trees as they gathered in the September dusk.

"It's so quiet," said Martha.

"Yes," said James, "I like it."

"I don't."

"Oh, Martha!"

"No, I don't like it. I hate it."

"Hush! Don't let them hear you." James lowered his voice to a whisper. "Why don't you like it?"

"I don't have any friends here. There's nothing to do. And besides, I just don't like it, that's all."

"Please, Martha, please don't let them know."

"Oh, for goodness sakes, James. Honestly!"

"I mean it, Martha."

"Why do you have to be so goody-goody all of a sudden?"

"I'm not, Martha. I'm not. But it is for us they wanted this house. I remember when we were little. All the time Daddy was in Med School and interning up north, and after we moved to the house downtown, I used to hear them talking at night. They thought I was asleep. It was all they talked about—how they wanted a house and yard, flowers and swings and a sandbox."

"Honestly, James, honestly!" That was

Martha's favorite expression. "What good will a sandbox do us? I'm eleven and you're almost thirteen."

"Jakie can have the sandbox. But I'm to have a private room. That's why I like the house. You've always had a room to yourself because you're a girl."

"It's friends I'm missing—Sally Ann and Nita. They were always there, one on one side and one on the other. When Sally Ann couldn't go with me some place, Nita could; and now they've got each other for friends and I don't have anybody."

"Mother's promised you a party when we get the house straight. You just keep your feelings to yourself. We're all going to like it when we get used to it. You're just spoiled, that's what!"

"What do you mean—spoiled?"

"You know what I mean. A room to yourself doesn't mean anything. You've always had a room. You never even had to wear hand-me-downs like Jakie."

"Oh, hand-me-downs! Hand-me-downs!

Jakie doesn't care about clothes. But we even live in a hand-me-down house!"

"Oh, Martha, that's silly. Almost everybody lives in a house that belonged to somebody. Very few people can afford new houses. And besides, Daddy says this old house is much better built than the new ones they are building nowadays."

"That's not what I mean."

"I know what you mean."

Silently they sat side by side for a few minutes swinging very slowly. There was a new sense of companionship between them.

After a while Martha asked, "Who lives there?" She motioned behind her.

"Mail carrier. I don't know his name. His wife teaches school. No children. I don't know who lives on the other side."

"It's not vacant. There are curtains at the windows."

As if in response to their wondering, an elderly lady came out while they were watching. She had on a fresh summer dress and an apron. She had a broom in her hand, and very slowly and painstakingly she began to sweep the porch.

Martha whispered to her brother, "Do you see what I see?"

"Yes," James replied, "she's white."

"Mother didn't tell me. Did anybody tell you?"

"No, but we knew it was a changing neighborhood when we moved in."

"Now," said Martha, "do you see what I mean?"

"You didn't even know about that when you said you didn't like it."

"No, but that's one reason why I don't like it. Sally Ann and Nita have been my friends forever—one on either side. Now I've traded them off for a schoolteacher and a mail carrier with no children and an old white lady."

As Martha and her brother watched her through the low-hanging branches of the trees, the old lady swept her porch slowly and carefully—sweeping the day's dust down toward the end of the porch just opposite their own.

James said nothing, but Martha continued

her whispered grumbling, "Now I ask you, who comes out to sweep the porch this time of day? Nobody. She just wanted an excuse to look at us. That's all. Well, I hope she's satisfied!"

"Sh! Don't let her hear you."

By this time their neighbor with the broom had gathered together a tiny pile of dust just inside the railing at the end of the porch. With one final push of the broom she swept the dust under the railing and it landed on the ground below.

"There," said Martha, "that shows what she thinks of us!"

"Oh, Martha," said James, "you mustn't talk like that. She has a right to come out and sweep her porch."

James looked up just as the lady finished her task. He thought there was a trace of a smile about her lips as she looked at him. But he couldn't be sure. He could not see very well through the branches of the trees. As he and Martha sat in silence, she turned and went into the house.

"Now," asked Martha, "do you see why I don't like it?"

"Yes. Is that the only reason?"

"No. We can't afford things."

"What things?"

"You know what things. Can we have a television? No. We've got a house. We've got to pay for the house. We want English bicycles. Can we have English bicycles? No. We've got a house. We've got to pay for the house. I want a desk for my room. We can't afford that either. When we moved, Mother gave away that old wreck of a sewing machine. But have you seen a new one around any place? I haven't. We can't afford it. We've got to pay for the house."

"Oh, Martha, you're the limit." James got up to go in the house. He opened the screen door with a jerk, then remembering his neighbors in time, he closed it softly behind him. But Martha followed him through the door and slammed it hard.

The furniture and rugs were in place, but in the living room were cardboard boxes full of books. In the dining room were barrels of china and in the kitchen were more cardboard boxes filled with pots and pans.

Their father was standing at the kitchen counter. He had served applesauce from a can on three plates. Now he was busy spreading peanut butter on bread for sandwiches. Suddenly Martha felt sorry for him.

"I'll do that for you, Daddy. Where is Mother?" she asked.

"She fed Jakie early," he answered, "and gave him a bath. I think they are both fast asleep."

James was searching through the boxes for some spoons for the applesauce. Martha poured milk into glasses to help her father, and then they all sat down at the kitchen table to eat their supper. It was their first meal in the new house, but it was strangely quiet and lonely without Jakie and Mother.

Afterward James and Martha went up quietly to their rooms. Martha shut the door and switched on the light. Her bed had been freshly made and her pajamas were lying ready where the sheets were turned back. She noticed that her mother had chosen a pink spread to match the gay flowers in the wallpaper. Against one wall were some boxes neatly stacked. These she knew contained books and clothes and odds and ends she could unpack and arrange herself.

In the corner by the front window was a surprise. A card table had been covered with a dark green plastic cover and on the fresh table top was a matching desk blotter. To the back of the table on one side was a pair of bookends and on the other side a student lamp. The card table was an old one, but the cover was new, and the blotter and the bookends and the lamp were all new. Beside this homemade desk and under the window was a bookshelf to hold Martha's schoolbooks and her favorite stories.

Martha opened the door to the hall. Across the hall the door to her parents' room was standing open. She walked over and stood for a moment in the doorway.

"Come in, dear," her mother said, "I'm not asleep."

"Thanks for the desk, Mother. It was sweet of you to fix me up so nicely."

"I think it will do very well until we can get you a real one."

Martha's father called softly from downstairs, "Good-night. I'll try to be in by ten, but don't wait up for me. It may be later than that."

Suddenly Martha turned and flew down the stairs. Her father put down his bag just as she flung herself into his arms. She knew he would not be in by ten. It would be closer to eleven-thirty or even twelve. At the end of this long tiring day he was going back to see a steady stream of patients. It was mostly maids and factory workers and men who did hard, hard jobs who came in the evening. Martha knew that her father cared about the problems of these people. They were indeed his people. There were others, too, who were his patients —old ladies with high blood pressure and babies whose mothers brought them for shots and regular checkups. These came, Martha knew, mostly during the morning office hours.

Long after the last weary patient would leave tonight, he would stay, checking his records and running tests in the lab.

Suddenly Martha was ashamed of her selfishness. She hid her face in her father's coat. She could not bear to have him see her cry.

"Good-night, sugar loaf," he said. That had always been his pet name for her.

"How about washing up those few things in the kitchen? And try to find us enough dishes and things for breakfast."

She was glad he had given her something to do. "I will, Daddy. Don't work too hard."

When he had gone she did as he had asked, but once again in her room upstairs, the old thoughts took possession.

"It looks like a desk," she thought, "but it still is just a card table. James said I was spoiled. I think he's the spoiled one. He's got a desk. He's got a real desk. James has always had a rcal desk."

Chapter 2

The next day was Saturday. There was cinnamon toast on the table when Jakie and Martha came running downstairs.

Mother went to the back door and called, "Breakfast is ready!"

James and Daddy came in from the yard and they all sat down in the dining room.

"Oh, boy," said James, "bacon and eggs and cinnamon toast!"

"I thought a real breakfast would taste good for a change," laughed Mother. "We've had so much dry cereal and applesauce and peanut butter since we started packing to move, I thought it was time for some real food again."

"And flowers," said Daddy. "Mary, where did you find the goldenrod?"

Mother laughed, and suddenly Martha felt as gay as the golden sun that fell across the yellow flowers on the table. She knew this was to be a happy day.

"We need a good breakfast," Mother was saying. "There is work to do for all of us. Clumps of goldenrod are blooming out by the back gate. They are the only flowers I could find. There are nothing but weeds in the flower beds."

After a pause for the blessing Daddy said, "Well, what are everybody's plans for today?"

James did not want to work in the yard. Martha did not want to work in the yard, and Jakie was too little to know what the others were thinking. He was the first to answer.

"I'm going exploring," he said.

Mother laughed again.

"It's perfectly obvious what I'm going to do. I'm going to unpack boxes."

"I'm going to unpack my boxes too," said Martha.

"Me, too," said James.

They all laughed then. Everybody knew what Daddy had on his mind—tall grass and weeds. That is, everybody knew except Jakie.

He didn't know what Daddy had on his mind, and he didn't care, either. Jakie had his own plans.

"As I've said before," said Jakie in his droll way, "I'm going exploring." And before anyone could stop him, he was out the back door and halfway across the yard.

"Come back here, Jakie," his mother called.

His father jumped up from the table and called after him, "Whoa, there, Jakie boy, where are you going?"

"Exploring," said Jakie as he looked up from the bottom step of the porch. His whole family were looking down on him from the kitchen doorway.

James looked at Martha.

Martha said, "I think I know where Jakie's going. He wants to see that little dollhouse in the back yard next door."

"It is not a dollhouse. It's a clubhouse," Jakie argued. "I bet I'm late already. I bet they're there now. I bet they meet every Saturday morning."

James said then, "He's just making that up."

Jakie insisted, "I am not making it up. They've got a porch and windows and everything. It's just like the big house. It would be a dollhouse for girls. But I bet it's a boys' clubhouse. There is a path to the club right through our fence."

"He means the fence is down in a hole through the hedge and the honeysuckle has grown up around it down there beyond the apple tree," James explained.

"Yes, James, I know," said his father. "Jakie, come here."

Jakie came up the back steps reluctantly. His father put his arm across his shoulders as he explained, "Jakie, nobody lives next door but an old lady."

"Yes, an old white lady," said Martha.

"Don't interrupt, Martha," said her father, and he continued, "Her husband is dead. Years ago she probably had some children. Maybe they are grown and married now. I don't know. Maybe they live far away. Perhaps she

has grandchildren who come to see her sometimes and play in the little house. But not very
often, not every day."

"It looks like new," said Jakie.

"Yes, she has kept it repaired and painted.
She probably had her own house and the little
house painted just this summer."

"Did she know I was coming? Maybe she
had it painted just for me."

"It's hopeless, Daddy," said James, as they
all started laughing.

"What's so funny?" asked Jakie. "Why is
everybody laughing at me?"

"Listen, Jakie," said his mother, "you may
go exploring if you want to. You may look at
the little house from our yard. You may go out
in the alley and look at the back of it. You may
walk all around the block on the sidewalk in
front of the houses. If you see some friendly
children you may invite them home with you.
But you must not go into anybody's yard. Is
that clear?"

"Yes, ma'am," he said, as he started around
the house toward the front sidewalk.

After Jakie had gone Daddy said, "Nobody asked me for my plans."

"We know your plans," said Mother.

Then James and Martha chanted together, "You are going to the hospital!"

"Yes," Daddy laughed. "I have to make rounds at the hospital, but after that I'm going shopping."

"For what?" asked Martha.

"That's to be a surprise."

"For whom?" asked James.

"It will be a surprise for everybody, but I must confess it will be a present for me."

Martha thought surely this was some kind of a joke. Surely her daddy would not buy a present for himself. She could never remember his buying a present for himself.

James was curious too, but too proud to show it.

"Excuse me," he said, "I'm going to unpack my things."

"Bring all the trash down," Mother cautioned him, "but save the good boxes. We'll need them in the attic."

Martha stayed to dry the dishes and then she went upstairs. James had unpacked his books and a big box of Scout equipment. His tent and his tent poles and his sleeping bag were piled up on his bed.

"Where in the world are you going to put all that stuff?" his sister asked.

"I'll manage. I'm going to roll it all up neatly first."

Martha walked to the center of the floor and sat down on the one box left for James to unpack.

"Martha!" James screamed at her. "Get off that box! That's my microscope."

"Oh," said Martha, standing up slowly. "Why didn't you tell me?"

"You knew very good and well I packed my microscope and slides in that box. I saved it for last to unpack because it has all that crumpled newspaper inside."

"I didn't hurt your old microscope. See? I didn't even make a dent in the box. Well, I guess I can tell when I'm not wanted." She sauntered off to her room.

In a few minutes she called out frantically, "Mother, Mother, come up here!"

"I'm busy, Martha. What's the matter?"

"My closet's not big enough."

"Not big enough! It's as big as any other closet."

"It's not big enough for me."

"Of course it is, Martha. You don't have that many clothes."

"It's full, and I haven't hung any dresses in it yet."

James called from his room, laughing, "Don't pay any attention to her, Mother. It's those crinolines!"

"I just hung up three crinolines and they took up the whole closet."

"Put your petticoats in the dresser drawers, Martha, and don't bother me again. I'm busy in the kitchen."

"There's not as much room in the dresser drawers as in the closet. Oh, well, I'll manage somehow!"

After a while she came to James's door again.

"James, will you lend me three sheets of typing paper and some Scotch tape?"

"I guess so, but don't use all my Scotch tape. I may need it myself."

After a while Martha came out of her room and went downstairs. She had hung her dresses in the closet. She had put her underwear and pajamas, sweater, socks, and toilet articles in the dresser drawers. Everything was in order. Against one wall, stacked neatly one upon another, were three very large packing boxes. On the side of each brown box a sheet of white paper was neatly taped. In black crayon on each sheet was printed this sign:

PRIVATE PROPERTY

CONTENTS: ONE CRINOLINE, STIFFLY STARCHED

DO NOT BUMP, RATTLE, POKE, OR OTHERWISE DISTURB

Chapter 3

Meanwhile, Jakie had gone exploring. He had been around the block on the front sidewalk. He had seen five squirrels and three dogs. He had seen two men who were mowing grass and one baby in a playpen in the morning sunshine. Jakie had watched for children his own age. He had seen four boys and three girls. He had said "Hi" to each one and each one had said "Hi" back to him. He had not been in a single yard, and now he was back on his own front walk.

Jakie did not come into the house. Instead he walked around to the back. He was still exploring and had saved the best place for last.

At the back of Jakie's yard, half hidden from the house by the garage and the overhanging branches of an apple tree, was a tangle of honeysuckle. It had completely leveled the wire fence that had once formed the boundary between the Andersons' property and the adjoining lot. Here Jakie had discovered on moving day a green tunnel leading straight through to the little white house.

Jakie stopped when he was exactly halfway through the tunnel. An old rotten fence post leaned away from the path against the green tangled vines. Jakie felt around with his foot until he found the hole where the post had been. Then he sat down on the path and put his heel in the edge of the hole. In this way he could be sure he was in his own yard, but he had a very clear view of the little house.

For a long time he sat there just looking. He was facing the side window. There was a window on the other side and a door in front opening onto a tiny porch. On either side of the porch step was a tiny flower bed. Pink petunias were spilling over the edge of the porch onto the grass in front. The house contained one room about eight feet long and six feet wide. The little house was a charming miniature of the big house, newly painted white clapboard trimmed in dark green.

As Jakie sat looking and dreaming, the owner of the house came across the grass. She had a little vase of water in her hand. She stooped to pick a few petunias and put them in the vase. She put the vase down on the porch and then she gathered a few seed pods from the straggling dry stems and put them carefully in an envelope which she took from her apron pocket. Then she picked up the vase and stooped to go through the little door. Jakie stood up then to look through the little window and see what she would do with the flowers. He saw her put them on a tiny table. Jakie could see that there were chairs in the house, two rockers and two straight chairs at the table. There were several pictures hanging on the walls. As Jakie watched her the old lady moved a chair slightly, straightened a picture on the wall, and then looked out the window straight at him!

"Hi," said Jakie. He had to say something and he didn't know what else to say.

"Hello! What's your name?"

"Jakie Anderson. What's yours?"

"Mrs. Hamilton. Wait a minute. I want to talk to you."

When she came out of the house, Jakie said, "I'm on my side."

"I see you are. Do you like my little house?"

"I don't know yet. I think I do, but I haven't seen it all."

"Would you like to see it?"

"Yes."

"Well, come on over."

"No, thank you."

"All right, suit yourself."

When she had gone, Jakie turned sadly and walked slowly across the lawn. He knew he had hurt Mrs. Hamilton's feelings. He couldn't be sure whether he had done the right thing or not. It was very hard to decide whether it was worse to hurt his neighbor's feelings or to disobey his mother.

Suddenly he realized he was very hungry. With two or three leaps like those of a flying squirrel he was up the high back steps and in the kitchen.

"Where is everybody?" he shouted. "I'm starved."

Daddy came home at last with the surprise. The car trunk was standing open to make room for a beautiful new power mower to cut the grass. Dr. Anderson and James read the instructions over and over. At last they filled the tank with gasoline and took turns as they cut the high neglected grass.

Martha walked around the new machine just once. Then she went up to her room, where she was busy all afternoon. Before supper her mother came upstairs and knocked on her door.

"Come in."

Martha was busy at her desk writing letters. Her mother lay down on the bed.

After a moment of silence Mother said, "I know how you feel."

"You know how I feel about what?"

"About the power mower. You were in hopes it would be something else."

"How could I? Daddy said it was to be a present for himself."

"Yes, but you didn't really believe it. He never buys a present for himself."

"Why do we have to talk about it?"

"We don't if you'd rather not."

"Go on. Get it over with."

"Your Daddy never buys a present for himself. You know that. He worked very hard to get his education after the war. At first everything he could spare after he started his practice had to go back into equipment for his office and lab. Then he bought this house for us. He works hard in his office and he is active in the church. He takes little trips with us sometimes. All these things give him pleasure. But he has never had a hobby. Do you know what he has always wanted to do?"

"No."

"He wants to have a garden. He wants to grow vegetables and flowers—especially roses. He needed the power mower to cut the grass quickly and easily so that he could have some time to work the garden and the flower beds. He loves the good brown earth. He grew up with it."

"I thought Uncle Jacob was the farmer in the family."

Martha put down her pen and got up and walked to the window. She could see her father and brothers, who were busy working together in the yard. They had finished mowing the grass. Her father was cutting the honeysuckle away from the fence, and James and Jakie were piling it into baskets and hauling them out to the alley to put beside the cans of trash.

"Your uncle Jacob is the farmer in the family. Your father is the doctor. He wanted to be a doctor. But all these years when he has walked the hard clean halls of hospitals, and the dirty city streets, he has dreamed of a little place of his own. He wanted it for us, too— the house and the yard—but for himself he wanted the grass and the brown earth and the growing things."

Martha leaned her head on the windowsill and burst into tears.

"Why do I have to be so ashamed? Every night I have to be so ashamed of something!"

"Jakie's never ashamed, Martha."

"Why do you say that?"

"He's too little to feel ashamed of anything. It is part of growing up to recognize selfishness in ourselves. But it is not good to stay ashamed."

After her mother had gone to put supper on the table, Martha thought about what she had said. She did not put her prayer into words. It was just an asking feeling in her heart. But when she skipped downstairs to supper she was as gay as the golden mood of the morning.

"Jakie, boy," she said, when he sat down at the table, "what were your adventures?"

Jakie told some of them, but not all, and not the most important.

Finally he said, "I didn't go in anybody's yard. I just looked in. But if I'm invited in sometime, would it be all right to go into somebody's yard sometime, just for a little while?"

They all laughed, and Mother said, "Of course, Jakie."

This time he did not say which yard he meant, and nobody asked him.

Chapter 4

The bright September days followed one another until suddenly there was the fragrance of fall in the air.

Everybody was busy. School began, and with it, Scout meetings and camping trips for James and music lessons and choir practices for Martha. Even Jakie, who had started in the second grade, was for a while too busy playing with his school friends to think much about the little white house next door.

Then, one afternoon when he was playing alone by the back fence, he saw Mrs. Hamilton again. She was kneeling on the ground in front of the little house planting pansies in the tiny flower beds.

"Hello!" said Jakie.

"Why, hello, Jakie. I haven't seen you for a long time."

"I've been busy."

Mrs. Hamilton laughed.

"Do you have homework in the second grade?"

"No, but I've been busy."

"You never came to see my little house."

"No."

"Would you like to see it now?"

"Yes, ma'am."

"Well, come on, then. I'll show it to you."

The old lady and the little boy went through the door together. Jakie saw the flowers on the little table. He sat in one of the straight chairs. He tried out a rocker.

"Boy, this sure is a neat house. It sure would make a fine clubhouse. Who uses it?"

"Nobody uses it now, Jakie. I keep it clean and straight because it would make me very sad if it came tumbling down. It helps me to remember . . .

"Well, once it was a dollhouse. That was when my girl was little. Then it was a clubhouse for her friends. Later, when she outgrew it, my son used it for his club. Then he used it for a meeting place for his Scout patrol."

"Are they your children?" Jakie pointed to the pictures.

"Yes."

"Where are they now?"

"My daughter has a little girl, but she lives far away. My son . . ."

"Where is he?"

"He was killed in the war. Now, run along, Jakie. You may come again some morning when I'm cleaning up in here."

Jakie still lingered.

"Mrs. Hamilton?"

"What is it, Jakie?"

Jakie stammered a little, and then he said, "May I show it to my sister, Martha?"

"I must go in the house, Jakie. Here is the key to the little house. You go get your sister, and when she has seen it, you lock the door and bring me the key."

"Oh, thank you, Mrs. Hamilton." Jakie took the key, and clutching it tightly in his hand he ran home as fast as he could.

Martha was setting the supper table when Jakie came running into the house.

"Martha, Martha," he whispered, "come here."

"What for?"

"Do you want to see it?"

"See what?"

"The little house."

"I've seen it."

"No. I mean inside. I've got the key."

"The key? What are you talking about? Mother-r-r!"

"Shut up, stupid." He began to whisper. "Mrs. Hamilton said I could show it to you, then I'm to lock the door and give her back the key."

"Oh, Jakie, well, sure, you know I want to see it."

Martha was tall for eleven and she had to stoop slightly to get in the door, but once inside she could stand upright.

"Oh-h-h!"

Martha looked around. She saw everything. She noticed things Jakie had not even seen: the pretty oval braided rug on the floor and the curtains at the windows.

"Isn't it neat, Martha? Isn't it the neatest thing?"

"What does she use it for?"

"She doesn't use it."

"What does she do with it?"

"She just takes care of it."

"Does anybody play in it?"

"Not now."

To Martha the most amazing thing about the house were the pictures on the walls. One showed a boy and girl playing together in a sandpile. It was an enlarged snapshot. The boy had on overalls and the girl had her hair cut straight across the front in bangs. There were several other pictures of the girl as she grew older, and there was a picture of the boy in his Boy Scout uniform and next to that a picture of him as a man in an army uniform.

"He's dead," announced Jakie.

"How do you know?"

"She said so."

"Oh, Jakie, let's get out of here."

Martha flew out the door and through the hole in the fence.

"Martha! Martha!" Jakie called after her. "I've got to take the key back. Don't you want to tell her 'thank you' for letting you see . . ."

But Martha didn't hear Jakie. She was already at home.

Later, at the supper table, Jakie announced, "Martha sure is a scaredy-cat."

"I am not!"

"She's even scared of a dead man's picture."

"I am not!"

"Why did you run, then?"

Dr. Anderson looked up.

"What is this all about? What dead man's picture? What are you two talking about?"

James said, "It's probably something Jakie made up. He's always making things up."

"I am not."

"I am not scared of a dead man's picture, either," said Martha.

"Then why did you run?"

Mrs. Anderson said then, "Please, children, begin at the beginning and tell us what this is all about."

"I'll tell you, Mother. I was not scared of

a dead man's picture. I can't explain it so Jakie will understand. It gave me the creeps."

"I told you she was scared." Jakie got in one last word and ran out of the room.

"What gave you the creeps?" asked her father.

"Well, it wasn't the picture. It was all that fresh paint and the flowers and the garden, and everything—everything new and fresh for children who aren't there any more. I can't explain it, I tell you. It just gave me the creeps."

Jakie came running in with a little package wrapped in newspaper.

"Daddy," he said, "it's almost dark. I've got to plant my flower garden. Will you please come out and show me where I can have my flower garden?"

"What have you got there, Jakie?"

"Pansy plants."

"Where did you get them?"

"Mrs. Hamilton gave them to me. She gave them to me when I took the key back."

"Did you say 'thank you,' Jakie?" asked his mother.

"Yes, I did. I said 'thank you' for the plants. I said 'thank you' for letting me see the house. I said 'thank you' for everything. But Martha didn't. She didn't even say 'thank you' for letting her see the house. She's a scaredy-cat. She's scared of a dead man's picture. She's scared of the little house. She's even scared of Mrs. Hamilton."

"I am not scared of a dead man's picture. I am not scared of Mrs. Hamilton. That house just gave me the creeps, that's all. Jakie doesn't understand."

"No, I don't understand, Martha. But I like Mrs. Hamilton."

"Come on, now, Jakie boy," said his father. "Let's plant those pansy plants."

"I'm coming, Daddy," and as he went through the kitchen after his father Martha heard him say as if to himself, "And I bet she likes me."

Chapter 5

One afternoon in early November, Martha came in from school and dropped her books in the hall.

"Martha," James called from upstairs, "what have you been doing? I've been home ages."

"Oh, this and that. Where's Mother?"

"She's not here. She's at church setting up tables for the family night supper."

"Where's Daddy?"

"He's at the office. I've got to go to Scouts. You're to stay with Jakie until Daddy gets home. Mother said for you to do your homework and get yourself and Jakie dressed by the time Daddy comes for you. Mother will be at the church until time for the supper."

"Big orders. Where's Jakie?"

"In the back yard. Good-bye. I'll see you later."

James banged the front door, and Martha picked up her books from the floor and trudged slowly upstairs. There was always a kind of quiet sadness in the house when Mother was not there.

From the window in her room she could see Jakie darting here and there across the grass. Then he settled down to play under the spreading branches which hung over the fence from the apple tree in Mrs. Hamilton's yard.

Martha laid out her clean clothes and then she went to Jakie's room and got out a clean shirt and pants for him to wear to the supper. Then she sat down at her desk and began to do her homework.

In a little while Jakie came up the steps. "Martha!"

"Here I am, Jakie. Don't bother me. I've got to finish my work."

"Just a minute, Martha. Do you have much to do?"

"No. Now go away, Jakie, and let me finish."

"All right. I'll go away, but I want you to help me, Martha."

"Help you do what?"

"Never mind. I'll wait. But hurry, will you, Martha?"

Martha got up and shut the door. Jakie went sadly down the stairs. Martha went back to her books. She could hear sounds from the kitchen where Jakie was opening and closing drawers and cabinet doors. Then she heard the water running in the sink. It ran for a long time.

Martha was answering her social studies questions when Jakie came upstairs the second time.

"Martha, please come now. I need you."

"You need me for what?"

"To help me."

"To help you do what?"

"Martha, you know something? I mean, we always have something good at church but not seconds on dessert. We never get seconds on dessert."

"No, we never get seconds on dessert."

"But sometimes at home we get seconds on dessert."

"Yes."

"Don't you think it would be nice if we have something all ready—another dessert, I mean. When we come home tonight after the supper at church we can have seconds on dessert before we go to bed."

"What, for instance?"

"Apple pie."

"Apple pie! I don't think we have any apples."

"Oh, yes, we do. Some are all peeled. I peeled a lot, but I need you to help me."

"Jakie! Did you pick those apples off Mrs. Hamilton's tree?"

"No. Some of them fell in our yard."

"But they are Mrs. Hamilton's apples."

"Now, Martha, you know one old lady couldn't eat all those apples, and besides, they were in our yard."

"There weren't very many on the ground the last time I looked. Jakie, did you shake the tree so they'd fall in our yard?"

"Just a little, Martha. Come on. She won't care. But you've got to help me. I don't know how to make a pie."

Martha followed Jakie to the kitchen.

"Jakie! It doesn't take all those apples to make a pie. You've got about a bushel in the sink!"

"I tried to peel them, but the peeling's too thick."

Suddenly Martha was very busy. She measured out flour, shortening, and salt. She found the pie pans. Her mother had taught her how to make a piecrust. In a very few minutes she was rolling out the dough.

"How many apples have you peeled, Jakie? I have enough dough for about three pies."

"Three pies! Oh, goody!"

Martha put the piecrust in the pans and began to fill them with the sliced apples. She sprinkled the apples with sugar and spices and put two of them into the oven.

"Jakie, boy," she said, "I'll peel and slice enough for the other pie. You go upstairs and wash your face and hands. I laid out your clothes. We'll barely have time to get ready before Daddy comes. The pies can be cooking while we dress."

"Oh, thanks, Martha. Oh, boy! Oh, boy!"

As Jakie ran off to get ready for church Martha filled the third piecrust. Then she gathered up the peelings and cleaned the counter and sink. Soon the delicious fragrance of sugar and cinnamon began to fill the kitchen.

"I'm ready, Martha," Jakie called, as she ran up the stairs.

"Good. It will only take a minute for me to change my dress and comb my hair."

As their father came in, Martha and Jakie were coming down the stairs together.

"Um-m-m. Something smells delicious," said their father. "I almost wish we were eating at home. Come on. We're late already. I'm glad you're dressed."

Jakie and his father started out to the car.

"Just a minute, Daddy. I'm coming," said Martha.

She ran to the kitchen and opened the oven door. All three pies were done. The first two were slightly darker brown than the third one she had made, but none were scorched.

Quickly she snatched a pair of pot holders and lifted the pies out of the oven and put them on the drainboard to cool.

Jakie and her father were in the car. Martha shut the front door and ran quickly down the front walk to join them.

Chapter 6

When they arrived at the church Martha met several of her friends and was so busy chatting about school and scouting that she forgot about the pies. But Jakie didn't forget.

"Do you like apple pie, James?" he asked during the supper.

"Of course. Everybody likes apple pie."

"We don't have apple pie at church suppers, do we, James?"

"Sometimes."

"Not homemade, James."

"I guess not. Not tonight, anyway. We're having cupcakes. I saw them."

"Oh, I see."

Jakie was about to tell James about the pies at home when suddenly he remembered how he got the apples. Then he thought about pies. James was very much like his father and mother about things like that. Jakie decided to wait and let those pies be a surprise to everybody.

"What made you think about apple pie, Jakie?"

"Oh, I don't know. I just thought about it."

"Well, I like apple pie best with vanilla ice cream on it."

"Do we have any vanilla ice cream at home, James?"

"I don't know. Why?"

"I just thought about vanilla ice cream, that's all."

It was dark when they got home. As their father opened the front door their mother said, "Bedtime for Jakie; and Martha, you and James go straight to your rooms to finish your homework."

"Not quite yet, Mother," said Martha. "Jakie and I have a surprise."

The secret revealed itself. The fragrance of the sugared apples and spices filled the house.

Jakie said, "Apple pie for everybody. Martha made three of them!"

"Why, that's fine, Martha," said Daddy.

He and James and Jakie followed Martha to the kitchen.

"Just one minute," said Mother. "Don't cut those pies. We didn't have any apples in the house. Where did you get those apples, Martha?"

"I found them in the kitchen."

"Jakie, where did you get those apples?"

"I found them in the yard."

"Our yard, Jakie?"

"Well, yes, I mean, most of them."

"Did you shake Mrs. Hamilton's tree so that the apples would fall in our yard, Jakie?"

"I shook it a little, Mother."

"Did you reach over to the other side to get any of those apples, Jakie?"

"Well, a few."

Suddenly Mother took over. She put the three pies on a tray and covered them neatly with waxed paper.

"Martha," she said, "those apples belonged to Mrs. Hamilton. Since you have made them into pies we cannot return the apples, but you are to take these pies to her and tell her you are sorry you took them."

"That's not fair. I didn't take the apples. I just made them into pies. Jakie took them."

"He will go with you."

"Please," Martha pleaded, "please don't make me go."

"Martha, when you made the pies you knew the apples belonged to Mrs. Hamilton, didn't you?"

"Yes." Martha began to cry. "I was only trying to make Jakie happy. He brought the apples in and asked me to make the pies."

"Mary," said Dr. Anderson, "I'm not trying to interfere, but it does seem to me that Jakie took the apples. He should be the one to apologize."

"I'm not scared of Mrs. Hamilton!" Jakie reached for the tray. But it was too big for him to carry.

"I'll take it to the porch for you," said James.

Before her mother could protest, Martha quietly slipped out of the room. James and Jakie went out with the pies. When Jakie had rung Mrs. Hamilton's doorbell James handed him the tray and backed away. Before Mrs. Hamilton could get to the door there was only Jakie standing in the dark with the apple pies.

Martha was sitting at her desk when James came upstairs. She heard him open the door to his room and close it quietly behind him. She listened, but she did not hear Jakie at all. She tried to think about her work, but she had her mind on Jakie and the apple pies. Finally she finished her homework and put her books away. Still Jakie had not come.

She opened the door and crossed the hall to James's room.

"James! Where's Jakie?"

"Still apologizing, I guess. I left him on the porch with the pies."

"Don't you think you ought to go get him?"

"Why should I?"

"Maybe he needs you to help him."

61

"He can carry an empty tray home."

"Why do you suppose he's taking so long?"

"I don't know, Martha. Now go away. I've got all my work to do. I didn't get a chance to study this afternoon."

Martha closed James's door and went back into the hall. She paused there a moment listening and then went downstairs. Her father had gone and her mother was in the kitchen. She opened the front door and went out. Jakie was nowhere to be seen.

She called softly into the darkness, "Jakie!"

There was no answer. She sat down on the top step and waited a few minutes. Still Jakie had not come. Martha went down the steps and across to Mrs. Hamilton's yard. As she approached the house she could hear Jakie's laughter above the noisy conversation coming from Mrs. Hamilton's television set. At last Martha's curiosity got the best of her. She climbed the steps and peeped in the window. The blinds were slanted so that she could barely see through the thin curtain into the room.

Mrs. Hamilton was sitting in an easy chair with a plate of apple pie and ice cream on her lap. Jakie was on a footstool at her feet. He, too, had a big piece of pie with vanilla ice cream on it. Jakie's favorite TV program was on the air, and the little boy and the old lady were enjoying it together.

Martha tiptoed away and returned home to wait for Jakie.

When the doorbell rang she ran to answer it. She found Jakie stooping to pick up the heavy tray from the porch floor.

"Why didn't somebody come to help me? I had to carry our two pies home all by myself."

James and Mother were standing in the hall.

"Well, at last! What have you been doing?" asked James.

"What do you think I've been doing? Eating apple pie and watching TV. What else do you think I've been doing? Mrs. Hamilton sure must think we're stupid! She says to tell you, Mother, that she can't possibly eat three pies. She says to tell you, Martha, that you are smart for eleven, to be able to make such good pies, and she told me that she can't possibly use a whole tree of apples either. I am to pick all I want in my yard, in her yard, on any branch that grows on that old tree. Here are your pies. I'm going to bed. I can't possibly eat any more pie tonight!"

"Mother," said Martha, "do we have any vanilla ice cream?"

"No. I'm sorry."

Martha sat down with Mother and James, and the three of them enjoyed their pie together. But Martha never did quite understand how things happened the way they did. It did not seem fair to her that Jakie, who took the apples in the first place, was the only one in the family who had ice cream with his apple pie.

Chapter 7

On the Friday before Thanksgiving it was almost dark before Martha came home. She had been to choir practice.

"Mother!" she called as usual when she came in. "I'm so tired."

"I know," said her mother. "Supper will soon be ready and there is no homework for tonight."

Martha was carrying her schoolbooks and a paper-wrapped bundle on top of them. She dropped her books on the table and took the bundle into the kitchen.

"It's no use, Mother. I'll just have to drop choir."

"Why?" asked Jakie. "I thought you loved it."

"Don't talk with your mouth full." Jakie was munching one of Mrs. Hamilton's apples.

"You don't have all that homework, Martha," called James from the living room. "Not on Fridays."

"It's not homework."

James came into the kitchen. "She's got some other reason, Mother. It sounds to me as if she's being temperamental or something."

"It's none of your business!" Martha took her little bundle and ran upstairs.

No one mentioned choir during supper, but later in the evening her mother went up to talk to Martha. Jakie watched from his bed as his mother went into Martha's room and closed the door. Then he slid out of bed, crossed the hall, and sat down very quietly on the floor outside Martha's room. This is the conversation that he heard:

"What is it about choir, Martha?"

"Nothing. Nothing at all."

"There must be something, Martha. Did you misbehave at practice? Did anyone say something to hurt your feelings?"

"No, Mother," said Martha, very patiently. "I have to give up choir, that's all. The reason is very simple. There it is in that brown paper lying on the bed."

Her mother opened the package.

"Why, Martha! This is lovely. You're going to have new robes—maroon and white."

"Take another look, Mother. That is not a choir robe. It has been measured to fit me. It has been cut out. But it is still just material. The mothers are making the robes."

"Why, that's fine, Martha. I'll be glad to make the robe for you."

"Mother, have you forgotten something? You don't have a sewing machine!"

"Is that all that's worrying you? I can easily baste it and take it into town and use someone's sewing machine to do the big seams. Now you stop worrying about choir. Come downstairs for a little while. Your dad's coming home early and maybe we can have some games before we go to bed."

"—But by Wednesday, Mother. I've got to have it by Wednesday. We are singing some Thanksgiving songs for the service that night."

"That doesn't give us much time, but we'll manage somehow."

Jakie scooted across the hall and was safely snuggled down under the covers when his mother came out into the hall.

The following morning Jakie was trying to build a hide-out with some old boards he had found in the alley behind the garage. He was hammering away happily when Mrs. Hamilton called to him.

"Jakie," she said, "I'm tidying up the little house for the winter. Would you like to come over and help me?"

Jakie dropped his hammer and nails among the boards on the ground and went across to meet Mrs. Hamilton. She was fitting the key in the lock.

"What do you want me to do?" he asked.

"There is not much to do, Jakie. Mostly I wanted your company. I like to talk to you."

"I like to talk to you too. What are we going to talk about?"

"You talk, Jakie. I'm going to sweep and dust and take the curtains down."

"Why are you going to take the curtains down?"

"Every fall I take the curtains and the chair covers and the little tablecloths and napkins into the big house. I wash and starch the curtains and I wash and iron the linens and chair covers and put them away in boxes until spring."

"Why?"

"I've always done it. I do it every fall."

"Why?"

"To make things fresh and clean. I put them back in the spring."

"Why?"

"I've always done it."

"Why?"

"Well, there is a reason. You see, there is no heat in the little house. When my daughter and son were young they played here in the spring and summer and early fall. When the days began to get very cold we liked to have them play in the sunshine when they were outdoors. The little house was usually closed up for the winter. When my little girl was old enough to take an interest in arranging things nicely we used to work together on it. Sometimes we made new curtains and pillows and tablecloths during the winter so that when spring came around again there would be some new furnishings for the little house. At Christmas time old Santa nearly always had something under the tree for the little house. One year he brought that little set of blue dishes. Another time he brought the little chairs over there . . ."

Jakie stood in the middle of the room just listening to Mrs. Hamilton and watching her as she gathered up the chair cushions and the tablecloth. She began to slide the curtains from their little rods.

"Oops, that one tore. I do believe these curtains are rotten. Well, I'll just have to make some new ones."

"Why?" asked Jakie again.

"You do love to ask 'why,' don't you, Jakie?" Mrs. Hamilton laughed.

"Well, I can't help but wonder. Martha says . . ."

"What does Martha say, Jakie?"

"Oh, nothing. Martha just says . . ."

"What does Martha say, Jakie?"

"She just says this little house gives her the creeps. I didn't mean to tell you that. It doesn't sound just right. Girls are funny, anyway."

Mrs. Hamilton didn't say anything and Jakie asked, "Did you say you are going to make some new curtains, Mrs. Hamilton?"

"Yes."

"Do you have a sewing machine?"

"Yes."

"Are you going to make the curtains on your sewing machine?"

"Yes."

"Why?"

"Well, why not?"

"You can't wear them."

"What are you talking about, Jakie? Of course you don't wear them. You put them up at the windows to make the house look pretty."

"But you can't do anything in them—like sing in the choir, for instance."

"Do you sing in the choir, Jakie?"

"No, but Martha does. She's going to sing next Wednesday—that is, she is if Mother gets her choir robe made in time."

"I'm sure your mother will get the new robe made in time."

"She could make it in a hurry if she had a sewing machine, but she hasn't one now."

"Oh, I see. Now I see. Do you think your mother would like to come over and use my sewing machine, Jakie?"

"I don't know. She doesn't know you very well—not as well as I do. She felt very bad about those apple pies. No, I don't think she'd ask you. She's got some kind of plan about taking it to one of her friends in town. But she didn't go today."

Mrs. Hamilton spoke softly, as if to herself, "I used to make choir robes for my little girl..."

"Would you, Mrs. Hamilton? Would you make it for Martha?"

"I would love to make the robe for Martha, but do you think your mother would like that?"

"Maybe, just maybe she won't know. You wait here. I'll be right back."

His mother was in the kitchen baking a cake for Sunday.

"Oh, boy," he said, "that smells wonderful. Chocolate! Where's Martha?"

"She's spending the day in town with Nita. Here, Jakie, I saved the icing bowl for you."

"Save it a few more minutes, will you, Mother? Please, will you? I'll be right back."

His mother looked a little startled. Never, never, had Jakie ever turned down a chance to lick the icing bowl. But she took him at his word and, asking no questions, she put the bowl and spoon back on the counter.

Jakie found the paper package on Martha's dresser just as she had left it. He snatched it up and stuffed it under his jacket.

Mrs. Hamilton was coming across her back yard with the little bundle of laundry when Jakie sauntered over to join her.

She smiled and said, "Come in, Jakie. I think it would be wise for us to discuss our business inside."

Once inside the kitchen they were both giggling like girls Martha's age with a secret.

"Did anybody see you?"

"No. Martha's gone to town and Mother's in the kitchen."

"It's beautiful material," said Mrs. Hamilton, as she opened the package.

"It's all cut out. Now you be very careful with it."

"Oh, I will, Jakie. I'll do a good job. You'll see."

"I'd better go back right away. Mother's saving the icing bowl for me. She might get tired of waiting and wash it. It's chocolate."

"All right. You run along. I'll see you later."

Jakie raced home, but before he had finished scraping the chocolate icing from the big mixing bowl, his friend next door was already at her sewing machine stitching the long seams of the lovely deep red cloth.

Chapter 8

Monday afternoon Martha called to her mother as soon as she came in, "Did you have time to . . . ?"

"Martha!" her mother interrupted. "What did you do with the choir robe? I was going to baste it up this morning and take it into town. I couldn't find it anywhere! What did you do with it? Sally Ann's mother was expecting me to come, and I finally had to call and tell her I couldn't find the material."

"It was right on my dresser this morning—no, it wasn't, either. I remember thinking it was there and I was going to remind you about it, but when I looked before school, it was gone. I didn't say anything because I just thought you had taken it somewhere else in the house to work on it. Are you sure it's not in your room?"

"I haven't touched it since Friday night,

Martha. I was planning to spend today on it. Where do you suppose . . . ?"

"I don't know."

Their voices got louder. Jakie was in the kitchen finishing the last bite of a sandwich.

He heard Martha say, "I wonder if Jakie . . . Jay-keee!"

But he was gone, racing across to Mrs. Hamilton's. In a few moments he returned sedately by the front door, holding a huge flat box carefully with both hands.

Martha and his mother were upstairs. He could hear Martha crying and trying to talk through her tears.

His mother was opening and shutting drawers and closet doors, and all the time trying to quiet Martha. "Now don't get so excited. We'll look everywhere first and ask James and Jakie. Then, if we can't find it, we'll get some more material. We still have two days . . . Hush, Martha, hush . . ."

By now Jakie felt very important. He walked slowly up the steps, holding the big box in front of him.

"Martha," he said very quietly, "I have a surprise for you. Which hand will you take?"

"Jakie! You had no right to tease me. Mother was going to make it today, and now this whole day is wasted . . ."

Then she saw the box. Slowly and wonderingly she took it from his hands. Mother came out of her room.

"You don't have to worry now. It's all made," Jakie said to her.

Martha opened the box. Inside was the choir robe. It was deep dark red with a gleaming white surplice. Mrs. Hamilton had made it beautifully. She had starched it slightly and ironed it. Then she had folded it so that not a wrinkle marred its lovely folds.

"Oh, Mother! Jakie, you little rascal!"

Martha was so relieved she began to cry again.

"Girls are so stupid! What are you crying now for?" Jakie asked.

"You wouldn't understand."

"There is nothing to cry about, Martha," said her mother. "We'll have to go thank her."

"Do I have to go?"

"Martha!"

Jakie started to tag along.

"Not this time, Jakie," said his mother. "You stay here."

But Jakie didn't mind. He could go to Mrs. Hamilton's whenever he wanted. Besides, he'd rather go by himself.

Later, when they were telling James and their father about the choir robe, Martha said, "James, she really is nice. You ought to get to know her."

"Well!" said James. "Look who's talking!"

Their father said gently, "Most folks are nice when you get to know them."

"She's nice, all right, but that little old house out back still gives me the creeps . . ."

James found himself again defending Mrs. Hamilton as he had done on moving day: "Well, it's her house, isn't it? I guess she's got a right . . ."

"Children, children, it's getting late now. Time for bed."

Chapter 9

"Martha!" called her mother. "Go outdoors and see if you can find Jakie. It is getting quite cold and he should come in now."

"Jakie!" Martha called from the porch.

"Sh, Martha, shh. Come here." His voice came softly out of the dusk.

"Where are you, Jakie?"

"Here I am around the side of the house. Come here, please."

As Martha went around the corner of the house she could see that her little brother was sitting down on the cold ground with his back against the bricks.

"Aren't you cold, Jakie? I'm freezing. Come on in."

"I can't. I can't come yet."

"What are you doing—just sitting there on the cold ground?"

"Nothing."

"You can't be doing nothing. You're never doing nothing."

"I'm just sitting here waiting for Mrs. Hamilton to come back and hang that curtain up."

"What are you talking about?" Martha looked where Jakie was pointing. The only light in the house next door was coming from an upstairs window. A white ruffled curtain was hanging diagonally against the pane as if one side of the rod were unfastened.

"She's getting that room ready for Christmas, Jakie. Her daughter's coming."

"I know. But that curtain has been like that all afternoon."

"She's probably gone somewhere. She'll be back. Come on. I'm freezing!"

"She didn't go anywhere. She knocked on that window and waved to me a long time ago. She was hanging that curtain then. I waved to her and then I went out back to play. When I came back again I couldn't see her but the curtain was still hanging like that. I'm just waiting. I'm not coming in until Mrs. Hamilton comes back to hang that curtain."

"That's silly. If you are so crazy about Mrs. Hamilton, why don't you just go and ring the doorbell?"

"I did. She didn't come to the door."

"Did you turn the knob?"

"Yes. It's locked."

"Did you try the back door?"

"It's locked, too."

"You see, Jakie, I told you she's gone away. Now come on in the house. You can go see Mrs. Hamilton tomorrow."

"She's in that house, Martha. She needs me. I know she needs me."

"Oh, Jakie. Well, come and tell Mother. She'll think of something."

"You know Mother wouldn't let me go in there when the doors are locked."

"You couldn't get in."

"I can get in. Come on."

Martha followed Jakie to the back of the

house. High up on the back porch wall was a little window. It was open.

"I can get in there if you will lift me."

"It's got a screen."

"I can break the screen."

"Mother wouldn't like that."

"I have to, Martha."

It was getting dark now. Martha lifted Jakie up and held him by the knees as he pushed out the screen with his fist. He scratched his face as he crawled through the little opening. A few cans came tumbling off the pantry shelf below the window and rolled noisily across the floor. There were no other sounds in the house.

Martha sat down on the back steps to wait. She drew her sweater closer around her body and hugged her knees. It was very cold, but she had to wait for Jakie. In a very few minutes she heard him call through the window.

"Martha, go home and call Daddy. Tell him to come right away. Get Mother. I'll meet her at the front door. Something terrible has happened to Mrs. Hamilton."

Martha ran like lightning. Her mother was slicing vegetables for a salad.

"Mother, come quickly!"

"Has something happened to Jakie? Has he hurt himself?"

"No. It's Mrs. Hamilton. He's with her. He told me to call Daddy too. Hurry, Mother. It must be something dreadful."

Her mother was wiping her hands.

"You go call your father, Martha. I'll go on over there."

Jakie met his mother at the door.

"Where is she?" she asked.

"Upstairs. She fell off the ladder while she was hanging the curtains. Mother, she won't talk to me. Where's Daddy?"

"He'll come. I know he'll come. Martha is calling him. You wait down here. I'll go and see if there is anything I can do for her."

Mrs. Hamilton was lying in a strange position on the floor by the window. Her feet seemed to be tangled in the rungs of the little stepladder, which had fallen over. She was still clutching the edge of the ruffled curtain.

Jakie's mother knelt by her.

"Mrs. Hamilton, can you hear me? I must call your doctor. Who is your doctor?"

"Dr. Brown. Dr. Preston Brown. It's my hip. Tell him I think I broke my hip. Jakie came."

"Yes. Jakie came. I'll go call your doctor."

She was dialing the number when Jakie came running in.

"Here comes Daddy," he said.

In no time at all an ambulance was at the door to take Mrs. Hamilton to the hospital. As she came downstairs on the stretcher Mrs. Anderson said gently, "Your doctor will meet you at the hospital, Mrs. Hamilton. We'll call your daughter and bring your things."

"Thank you," she whispered, before the ambulance door closed behind her. "Thank you for everything. Tell Jakie thank you."

Chapter 10

The first cold dreary days of December lengthened into weeks and suddenly there was the excitement of Christmas in the air. Every time James and Martha came in they went up to their rooms with mysterious bundles in their arms. They posted signs on their doors:

PRIVATE
KEEP OUT

Mother was baking fruitcakes and cookies and wrapping packages for the grandparents and cousins and aunts and uncles who lived in the country.

Jakie had secrets with his mother about his presents for the other members of the family, and he helped her with the cookie baking and decorating. The fragrance of orange peel and vanilla, of cinnamon and chocolate, filled the air.

Then one day there was added the smell of pine and cedar. It was time to decorate the Christmas tree.

Martha went about the house singing "Silent Night" and "O Little Town of Bethlehem." The days were filled with fun and the joy of anticipation, but for Jakie, something was missing. He felt so sorry for Mrs. Hamilton that he could think about very little else.

One day he asked his mother, "Have you ever been in the hospital for Christmas?"

"No, Jakie," she answered, "I don't believe I have."

"It's not much fun being in the hospital for Christmas."

"No, I guess not. I've bought a present for Mrs. Hamilton—a pink bed jacket from the family. But if you would like to give her a present all by yourself I'll take you to the greenhouse and we can pick out a pretty flower for her. Would you like that?"

"Come on, Mother. Let's go right now."

"Tomorrow will be time enough. That's the day before Christmas Eve."

The next day Jakie and his mother were returning from the greenhouse when the delivery man stopped in front of the house and took a television set from the back of his truck. Jakie was so excited he almost dropped the beautiful red poinsettia he had bought for Mrs. Hamilton.

"Oops!" said his mother. "That surprise came a little early. Well, we can enjoy the Christmas programs together."

Later in the evening their father explained, "You children must not expect big presents this year. The television set is the one big present we are all giving to each other. Is that all right?"

"That's just fine, Daddy," said James. "We all wanted TV."

Martha joined in, "Thanks a lot, Daddy. It's a wonderful present."

On Christmas Eve night as Jakie went upstairs he called, "Daddy, you didn't mean we won't have candy canes, did you, Daddy? We always have candy canes."

His father laughed. "Don't you worry,

Jakie, about the candy canes. I'm sure there'll be candy canes. Now you scoot on up to bed."

Jakie tried hard to go to sleep. But it was always hard to go to sleep on Christmas Eve. There was a great deal of whispering and giggling and rattling of papers. Finally Martha and James came up to bed. There was more whispering and rattling of papers. Then the doorbell rang.

Jakie heard his father say, "Come in, come in."

The visitor introduced himself. Jakie heard only the words, "Mrs. Hamilton's son-in-law."

Then he heard his father say, "Come on back to the kitchen where we can talk . . ."

There was more whispering, and then it was strangely silent in the house and Jakie fell asleep.

It was still dark when Jakie woke up. Martha was shaking his bed.

"It's Christmas, Jakie! Get up!"

Jakie sat up, rubbing his eyes.

"Mother says to tell you to get dressed in

warm clothes and put on your coat. Some of your presents are outdoors."

"Outdoors?"

"Don't ask any questions. Just hurry. Everybody's waiting for you."

Jakie was ready in a minute. His father and mother and James were waiting for him in the kitchen.

"Shall we have breakfast first?" asked Mother.

Jakie knew she didn't mean it. She had on her coat. His father was carrying a flashlight.

"Quit teasing, Mother," said Martha, opening the door.

"Are everybody's presents outdoors?" asked Jakie.

"No," said James. "We all have presents under the tree in the living room and stockings hanging up in there. But some of your presents are outdoors and we all want to see them."

Martha opened the door and Dr. Anderson followed with the flashlight. Jakie took his mother's hand. It was all very mysterious. He felt strangely unlike himself going out into the cold darkness.

"Maybe I haven't waked up yet," thought Jakie. "Maybe I'm still dreaming."

But it was no dream. His father and Martha led the way across the yard with the flashlight, and he followed with his mother. James held the shrubbery back and they all went through the hedge into Mrs. Hamilton's yard. Then his father shined the light on the little house.

"Look at the door!" said Jakie. "It's all wrapped up like a Christmas present."

Jakie ran on ahead then to the door of the little house. A big red ribbon tied the door like a package. In the middle of the door where the big ribbon bow was tied an envelope was attached, and on the envelope was printed in big letters: J A K I E.

Jakie took the envelope down with trembling fingers. Inside was a Christmas card. As Jakie took the card from the envelope he knew that there was something heavier than paper attached to it. Inside the folded card the key

to the little house was taped to the picture of a Christmas tree. On the opposite side was a note.

"Read it, Mother," said Jakie.

His mother read by the light of the flashlight:

Dear Jakie,

Merry Christmas. The little house, including all that you find in it on Christmas morning, is my Christmas gift to you. Your father and James will build a foundation for it, and as soon as they can, they will move it to your yard.

When I am well enough to travel I am going to live with my daughter. I will miss you. I hope you will enjoy the house and the little presents I have sent you. But I want you to know that nothing I could ever give you is as good as the gift you have given me.

With love from your friend,
Mrs. Hamilton

The biggest surprise awaited them in the house. It was beginning to be light enough to see. Jakie fitted the key in the lock and opened the door.

"Mother! Daddy! Martha! James! Look! It's different! It's all fitted up for a clubroom."

Indeed it was. There were no doll dishes or other girls' things. There were a few chairs just Jakie's size and some benches against the walls. In the center of the room was the table with a chair behind it, all ready for a president to take his place and call the meeting to order. On the table were some Christmas gifts wrapped in gay paper.

There were no pictures on the walls. There were no ruffled curtains at the windows. But the rugs were on the floor and the floor had been newly scrubbed and waxed. The windows were clean and shining. Somebody had worked hard to turn the beautiful little dollhouse into a clubhouse for a boy.

"Who changed it? Mrs. Hamilton is in the hospital. Who fixed it all up, Mother?"

"Mrs. Hamilton's daughter and her husband have been working on it ever since they came. They did it exactly as she told them. Mrs. Hamilton planned it herself for you, Jakie. Aren't you going to open your presents?"

It was all too much for Jakie.

"Are they for me too, Mother? Are they all for me?"

"Yes. Mrs. Hamilton had presents sent to all of us. Ours are in the house. These are yours."

Jakie was taking the paper and ribbons off.

"Oh, boy, a cook kit! An official Boy Scout cook kit!"

But that was not all. There was a flashlight. There was a pair of binoculars. There was a canteen to carry water on camping trips. There was a pocketknife.

"Some of these things are new, Jakie, but a few of them belonged to her son when he was a little boy. She has taken good care of them all these years. She wanted you to have them." His mother spoke quietly.

He handed the card to his mother.

"Read it again, Mother. Read it again, please."

His mother read the note through again. As she read the last sentence, "I want you to know that nothing I could ever give you is as good as the gift you have given me," Jakie listened very carefully.

"Mother, I didn't give Mrs. Hamilton anything—just that old red flower. Besides, I didn't even buy that with my own money . . ."

Martha laughed. "She wasn't talking about that!" Martha thought Mrs. Hamilton meant that Jakie had found her when she was injured and needed help.

James knew that Mrs. Hamilton meant more than that, but he could not put it into words. Silently he put his arm around his little brother's shoulders as they went out into the Christmas dawn. James knew that Jakie was the only one of them who had given Mrs. Hamilton the perfect gift of love. Somehow Jakie had given them all the gift of love.